T0380502

AuthorHouse™ UK
1663 Liberty Drive
Bloomington, IN 47403 USA
www.authorhouse.co.uk
Phone: 0800.197.4150

Published by AuthorHouse 04/02/2019

ISBN: 978-1-7283-8502-0 (sc)
ISBN: 978-1-7283-8503-7 (e)

Print information available on the last page.

Any people depicted in stock imagery provided by Getty Images are models,
and such images are being used for illustrative purposes only.
Certain stock imagery © Getty Images.

This book is printed on acid-free paper.

authorHOUSE®

The Lord with the Hunchback

There was once a lord who lived with his servants in a gigantic castle. He rented his land to the farmers. He greedily increased the rent each year by a large amount, and the farmers were unhappy. They told the lord the high rental price meant they and their families went hungry. All they earned went for the rent, so they had no money left to care for their families.

The farmers looked to the good fairy for help. The good fairy became angry with the lord and his greed. She punished him by placing a hump on his back. The good fairy told the lord, "You will carry this hump on your back from sunrise to sunset. It is a symbol of your greed. You will have pain because of your hump so you will understand the pain of the farmers. Only when you fall in love and that person loves you will this curse be lifted."

"I don't understand," replied the lord. "What does love have to do with liberation of this curse?"

"It will make you understand," she answered.

So he could only be freed of the hump when—and if—he fell in love with someone who loved him in return. He had little chance of deliverance from this curse because not everyone found such love.

After he received the curse, the lord sent away the old servants and hired new domestic staff. He began his new life with the new servants. He let employees collect the rent, and the farmers no longer saw the lord thanks to the good fairy's curse.

His hump forced him to bend at the waist, and he could not walk upright. His stoop made him look quite pathetic. The lord could not lie on his back, so he lay on his right side or his left.

Each morning, the lord received his cup of coffee in his office. By afternoon, his pain was worse, and he rested in his bedroom in the afternoon. His pain was so bad that he often lay in bed, moaning.

Despite the pain caused by his hump, the lord did not reduce the rent for his fields. He could not control his greed. The lord thought he did not have to lower the rent because he would be liberated when he fell in love with someone who also loved him.

After sunset, the lord went to the balls. No one knew he got his own form back from sunset to the sunrise. According to tradition, there was a monthly ball from sunset to sunrise. Everyone could meet and dance with each other. The lord of the castle rode his horse on the hidden path behind the castle to the ball. No one knew about that path, so he always rode alone. Huge thorns surrounded the path, but he was so charming that, after sunset, even the thorns changed into shiny roses to greet him. And since he was without his hump, no knew who he was, so he pretended to be someone else.

Months passed, and he still had not fallen in love, which was necessary to be liberated from the curse. No ladies at the balls fascinated him. He did find a number of them beautiful, but being captivated was something totally different. He understood that falling in love was beyond his control. He was at the point of giving up hope. He thought he would never fall in love. Even though he had no hope, he continued to enjoy himself at the balls.

One day, someone knocked on the castle door. The servant opened the door, and a young woman asked the servant if she could work there. When the servant consulted with the lord, he accepted her offer. The lord took her in under a certain condition: she was not allowed to ask questions.

***

This servant was named Juliana. Her tasks were cooking, cleaning, washing, and ironing. She worked from sunrise to sunset. After sunset, she returned to her farm, where her grandmother had died not long before. This farm had a stable. It was a magical stable.

As her grandmother was dying, she told Juliana about the magic of the stable and the magic of the wardrobe in her bedroom. After her grandmother's death, Juliana had to live on her own on the farm.

On her deathbed, her grandmother told Juliana she didn't need to be afraid. No evil act could take her because she had a pure heart.

"You have to go to the balls," she said, "so you need a ball gown. The wardrobe in my bedroom is magic. Before you open the wardrobe, wish for the kind of ball gown you want to wear. And in the stable, a carriage will be waiting for you."

Juliana quickly got used to working in the castle, but she found the castle and the lord very strange. The interior of the castle contained beautiful and valuable furniture, but during the day, the curtains were only half-open. Because the curtains partially covered the windows, the sun could not fully illuminate the rooms. Therefore, the castle didn't look lively.

This was the wish of the lord. In the daytime, Juliana always found him in a bad mood, and he wanted no sunlight in the castle. However, after sunset, he was so good-natured and even wanted to host balls to entertain himself.

One day, when Juliana was cleaning the lord's wardrobe, she was fascinated by the valuable fabrics used to make his chic costumes. She was surprised because she did not expect the lord, with such a sullen character, to go to the balls to entertain himself. Or was she mistaken? Would he really attend the balls?

If he did not attend the balls, why would the cleaning of his clothes be one of her duties? With all these questions in her head, she felt an intense curiosity and decided to go to the ball.

He was so mysterious, this lord. She didn't even know his name. She dared not ask him. She was not allowed to ask such questions; it was a condition of her employment.

Juliana had already asked the other servants, but they didn't know his name either. After all, they had all come to the castle after the lord had sent away the old ones after the good fairy had cursed him. They told her they were not allowed to ask his name either.

One day, she decided to ask him. She knocked on his office door and went in. Juliana found him so frightening that her heart was pounding. "Dear, Lord," she said, "I have worked here for a while, but I don't know how to address you." He got up from his chair, went to her, and looked into her eyes. He did not talk; his eyes spoke what he would have said. Juliana understood and nodded submissively. She left the office, her heart still pounding. She thought about the beautiful costumes she had seen in his wardrobe. *He probably wears them during the balls. They are certainly not everyday clothes,* she thought.

After several weeks, she received an invitation to the ball. Each month, everyone got an invitation. She decided to go to the ball to see the lord. But before she could leave for home, she had to light the fireplace. While the fireplace was heating, she said to the fire, "You are so nice and warm." After these words, the fire filled her with tenderness. After she was done, she went home.

Juliana stood before the door of the wardrobe in her grandmother's room and made a wish. "I would like to be stunning," she said before opening the wardrobe. When she looked inside, she saw a ruby-red ball gown with matching shoes and handbag. When she put on her magical ball gown, her hair took on a new style, and her face was made up. She even had ruby-red gemstone jewellery. She was unrecognizable because of her beautiful appearance. Her dress, shoes, handbag, and hairstyle were in perfect combination. Her makeup was radiant, allowing her beauty to be flawlessly expressed.

She went into the stable and opened the door. The carriage was waiting for her. Everything was in perfect order. One of the carriage riders smiled at Juliana and said, "Greetings from your grandmother in the sky." She smiled back and thought of her grandmother, and she was filled with gratitude.

When they arrived, Juliana took a deep breath to calm down. It was her first time at a ball. As she entered, all eyes were directed to her. Juliana was so beautiful that the entire ballroom was quiet as a mouse. Even the orchestra stopped playing. She greeted everyone gracefully, and the music continued.

Her curious eyes searched the ballroom for the lord. Then she recognized him. He was so charming that her heart was pounded. She noticed that he had no hump. *How mysterious*, she thought. Juliana felt she had done well to come to see him.

There was a great attraction between them, and they danced for hours. She felt as if the dance music had been composed for the lord and Juliana. The atmosphere surrounding their dance was so magical that everyone was impressed. The couple danced with great feeling. The evident great attraction between Juliana and the lord made the dance that much more meaningful to the spectators.

They enjoyed each other's company so much that they forgot to ask each other's names. The lord was impressed by her eyes, which seemed to speak without using words. The lord thought, *I have seen the same eyes and the same look, but on whom?* It was like a puzzle whose pieces had to be fit together.

After dancing, they went to the balcony to enjoy the night atmosphere under the stars. He noted how excited she was. "Why are you so excited?" he asked.

She thought, *What if he found out that I am his servant?* Her heart was pounding with excitement.

"Why are you so quiet?" he asked her. "You are so excited that I can hear your heartbeat," he said. They both laughed. Their laughter calmed her excitement.

She thought, *What if he recognizes me?* She looked into his eyes and said, "I am impressed with your charm."

He smiled. "If anyone is charming tonight, it's you," he said, emphasizing his words with kisses on her hands. She was so used to seeing him gruff during the day that she never thought he would ever smile at her. His smile could get so close to a person.

His smile also made her smile. She felt that not only her face but her eyes and heart smiled too.

At the end of the ball, they said their reluctant goodbyes. The atmosphere was so magical that they would never forget this night. They agreed to see each other again at the next ball.

It was like a dream come true for Juliana. She found the lord so charming and so different.

He was totally a different person tonight. During the day, he is so surly! she thought while she undressed in her home. She put her ball gown and accessories, such as shoes and handbag, back in the wardrobe. She was not aware of her incredible charisma, which had captivated the lord.

The next day, Juliana was so nervous that her hands were shaking as she poured the coffee. She let the coffee cup fall out of her trembling hands.

"Do I look so terrible?" asked the lord. He noticed her excitement. Juliana was silent. She didn't know what to say. She picked up the coffee cup and cleaned the coffee that lay on the floor. He noticed her graceful hands. He could not take his eyes off them. They were so graceful. It was as if he had seen them earlier. But where? He was confused.

That afternoon, the lord went to his bedroom. He felt intense pain in his hunchback. He groaned. Juliana happened to pass by the door of the bedroom, and she heard the lord groan. She could not stop her tears, so intense were her feelings. She found this castle and its lord so secretive, and yet she liked to work here because she saw the lord every day. She had fallen in love with him.

The days went by, and the ills and moodiness of the lord continued, but Juliana persevered. On one day, Juliana went to the flower garden to make a bouquet of flowers. Placing such a bouquet on the dining table was one of her tasks. A smile appeared on her face. Despite the lord's surliness, he wished to have a bouquet in a vase on his dining table. While she was working with the bouquet, she spoke with admiration of the nature around her. "You have such exquisite beauty."

***

The invitation for the next ball was distributed to the people. Everyone was excited to go. Juliana felt so relieved to receive an invitation that her eyes shone like stars. All the servants noticed how happy she was, but they did not understand why.

After sunset broke, the time for the ball had arrived. Everyone was curious as to whether the beautiful lady would come back. Without a doubt, her indescribable beauty would honour the ball's invited guests.

She stood before the door of the wardrobe and made a wish.

"I want to be as beautiful as Mother Nature," she wished before she opened the wardrobe. She saw an emerald green ball gown with matching shoes and handbag. She put on her ball gown, and the moment she did, her hair took on a new style and her face was adorned with makeup. She was even wearing emerald gemstone jewellery. She was unrecognizable because of her beautiful appearance. Her dress, shoes, handbag, and hairstyle were in perfect combination. Her makeup was radiant, allowing her beauty to be flawlessly expressed.

She went into the stable and opened the door. The carriage was waiting for her. Everything was in perfect order. One of the carriage riders smiled at Juliana and said, "Greetings from your grandmother in the sky." She smiled back and thought of her grandmother, and she was filled with gratitude. She took a deep breath to calm down. She was ready to go to the ball.

When she entered the ballroom, the invited guests watched her with admiration. Her presence changed the atmosphere of the ball. She didn't know that all eyes were directed to her. She greeted everyone gracefully. The music played.

Her curious eyes searched the ballroom for the lord. Then she recognized him. He was so charming that her heart was pounding. There was a great attraction between them, and they couldn't keep their eyes off each other. They danced for hours.

She felt as if the dance music had been composed for the lord and Juliana. It was as if the entire ball had been organized just for them. The atmosphere was so magical that everyone stopped dancing and watched the two of them. The invited guests enjoyed watching how they danced. The charm of the lord and the beauty of Juliana created the perfect, most magical atmosphere.

The lord was fascinated by her emerald green look. He whispered to her while dancing, "I can look at you for hours." Juliana felt happy. After dancing, they went to the balcony to enjoy the night atmosphere under the stars.

"In your presence, totally different feelings come to me, ones I could never describe," said the lord.

"To me as well," answered Juliana. "I have the same feelings in your presence."

It was as if they had been invited to love.

"What is your name?" he asked her.

"Juliana," she replied. "And you?"

"Armando."

They felt no distance between them. The hours flew past in each other's company, and too soon it was time to leave.

At the end of the ball, they said their reluctant goodbyes. They agreed to see each other again at the next ball. During the departure, the lord kissed her fingertips, full of adoration. He admired her beauty. The atmosphere was so magical that they would never forget this night.

I almost fainted in his arms from excitement while dancing, Juliana thought as she undressed at her home. She put her ball gown and accessories, such as shoes and handbag, back in the wardrobe. She felt thankful to her grandmother.

The next day, the lord enjoyed his breakfast. He drank his coffee with pleasure, without any of his usual surliness. The castle servants were surprised by his good mood. They all liked that he was not surly that day. They did not know it was because he was thinking of the beautiful Juliana of the previous night's ball.

After his breakfast, he went to the garden of the castle. It was the first time since the curse that he went out during the day to get fresh air. He was in such a good mood. Unfortunately, that afternoon, he had to go back to his bedroom because the pain in his back was intolerable. Because of his pain, his favour was short-lived, and he felt sad.

In the following days, he often went to the garden to get fresh air. His state of mind had changed thanks to Juliana's companionship during the balls, and he was looking forward to the next ball to see her. He had gotten used to her company. She had become a part of his life, a light in the darkness. The days went by with the ills and the moodiness of the lord and with the perseverance of Juliana.

The following ball invitation was distributed to the people. Everyone was excited to go. Juliana felt so relieved to receive another invitation that her eyes shone like stars.

The sun set, and it was time for the ball. Everyone was curious: would the beautiful lady come back? Without a doubt, her beauty added a fascinating atmosphere to the ball. As she danced with the charming castle lord, they would be a feast for the eyes of the invited guests.

After her tasks in the castle were complete, she went to her house. It was a busy day for her, but luckily she got home in time to get ready for the ball.

She stood before the door of the wardrobe and made a wish.

"I would like to shine like the stars in the sky," she wished. She opened the wardrobe and saw a sapphire blue ball gown with matching shoes and handbag. She put on her ball gown. Again, her hair styled itself and her face was adorned with makeup. She was even wearing blue sapphire gemstone jewellery. Thanks to her beautiful appearance, she was unrecognizable. Her dress, shoes, handbag, and hairstyle were in perfect combination. Her makeup was radiant, showing her beauty flawlessly.

She went into the stable and opened the door. The carriage was waiting for her. Everything was in perfect order. One of the riders of the carriage smiled to Juliana and said,

"Greetings from your grandmother in the sky."

She smiled back, and thought of her grandmother filled her with gratitude. She took a deep breath to calm down. She was ready to go to the ball.

The invited guests watched her with admiration as she entered the ballroom. Her presence added a fascinating atmosphere to the ball. Her eyes searched for the lord. She didn't realize that all other eyes were directed at her. She greeted everyone gracefully. The ball went on as the music played.

She recognized the lord. He was so charming that her heart was pounding. There was great attraction between them, and they couldn't keep their eyes off each other. They danced for hours.

It was as if the dance music had been composed just for Juliana and Armando. It was as if the entire ball had been organized just for them. The atmosphere was so magical that everyone stopped dancing and watched them as spectators. It was like a fairy tale, so magical, and the guests enjoyed it immensely. The charm of the lord and the beauty of Juliana completed the magical atmosphere of the dance.

The lord was fascinated by her sapphire blue appearance.

"You radiate so that even the stars are dull next to your appearance," said he to Juliana, filled with adoration.

After dancing, they went to the balcony to enjoy the night atmosphere under the stars.

"Why have I not seen you so far?" he asked innocently. She did not know what to say. "You know," he continued, "you are the first and last lady who has fascinated me." She smiled at him. "May I listen to your heartbeat?" he asked her with a smile.

She was surprised and nodded yes.

He put his ear next to her heart. Then he stood upright and said, "Your heart says you love me."

They both laughed. It was as if they had been created for each other.

The hours flew past in each other's company, but soon it was time to leave.

At the end of the ball, they said goodbye to each other reluctantly. They agreed to see each other again at the next ball. During the departure, the lord kissed the hands of Juliana, full of adoration. He admired her beauty. The atmosphere was so magical that they could never forget this night.

It was like a dream come true for Juliana. She found the lord so attractive that she could dance for hours in his arms.

He's so magical! thought Juliana as she undressed at her home. She put her ball gown and accessories, such as shoes and handbag, back in the wardrobe.

The next day, the lord went to the garden of the castle, as he had in the past few weeks. He saw in the garden that the new servant was sleeping.

Juliana had fallen asleep on the couch in the garden. He looked at her face. He knew that face from somewhere, but where? He was confused. Very quietly, he went back inside so as not to wake her. He seemed to feel her sleep was sacred and no one was allowed to wake her.

One day, when Juliana was in the garden, working with a bouquet of flowers, she said to the flowers, "You are so innocent."

The days went by with the ills and the moodiness of the lord and the perseverance of Juliana.

The invitation to the next ball was distributed to the people. Everyone was excited to go. Juliana felt so relieved to receive an invitation that her eyes shone like stars.

Sunset broke, and it was time for the ball. Everyone was curious: would the beautiful lady come back? Without a doubt, her beauty fascinated everyone in the ball. The charming castle lord and Juliana would present a feast for the eyes for the invited guests.

After her tasks in the castle were complete, she went home. It had been a busy day for her, but luckily she got home in time to make it to the ball.

She stood before the door of the wardrobe and made a wish.

"I would like to radiate innocence," she wished before she opened the wardrobe. When she opened the door, she saw a pearly white ball gown with matching shoes and handbag. She put on her ball gown, and her hair and makeup transformed. She was wearing pearly gemstone jewellery and a pearl necklace around her neck, with a pearl bracelet on her wrist, a pearl ring on her finger, and pearl earrings. She was unrecognizable because of her beautiful appearance. Her dress, shoes, handbag, and hairstyle were in perfect combination. Her makeup was radiant, showing her flawless beauty.

She went into the stable and opened the door. The carriage was waiting for her. Everything was in perfect order. The rider of the carriage smiled to Juliana and said, "Greetings from your grandmother in the sky."

She smiled back and thought of her grandmother, and she was filled with gratitude. She took a deep breath to calm down. She was ready to go to the ball.

The invited guests watched her with admiration as she entered the ballroom. Juliana was as a bride. Her mere presence made the ball worthwhile for the gathered guests. Her eyes searched for Armando. She did not know that all other eyes were directed at her. She smiled at everyone in greeting. The ball commenced and the music played.

She recognized the charming castle lord, and her heart pounded. There was a great attraction between them, and they couldn't keep their eyes off each other. They danced for hours.

It was as if the dance music had been composed for the lord and Juliana. It was as if the ball had been organized just for them. The atmosphere was so magical that everyone stopped dancing and watched the two of them as spectators. It was like a fairytale.

The lord was fascinated by her pearly appearance.

"Your beauty must have come from the planet Venus," he said as they danced.

After dancing, they went to the balcony to enjoy the night atmosphere under the stars.

"When I look in your eyes, I forget all my greed," said Armando.

"When I look in your eyes, I forget who I am," said Juliana.

"Who are you, anyway?" he asked her.

"Does it matter who I am?" she answered.

"No," he said, "whoever you are, I will always love you." Emphasizing his words with kisses on her fingertips.

The hours flew past in each other's company, and soon it was time to leave.

At the end of the ball, they said goodbye to each other reluctantly. They agreed to see each other again at the next ball.

It was like a dream come true for Juliana. She found the lord so attractive that she could have danced for hours in his arms.

He loves me! thought Juliana as she undressed at her home. She put her ball gown and accessories, such as shoes and handbag, back in the wardrobe.

The days went by with the ills and less moodiness of the lord and the perseverance of Juliana.

The next ball invitation was distributed to the people. Everyone was excited to go to the ball. Juliana felt so relieved to get an invitation that her eyes shone like stars.

Sunset broke, and it was time for the ball. Everyone was curious: would the beautiful lady come back? Without a doubt, her beauty fascinated everyone in the ball.

After completing her tasks in the castle, she went to her house. It had been a busy day for her, but luckily she got home in time to prepare for the ball.

She stood before the door of the wardrobe and made a wish.

"I would like to radiate sunshine," she wished before she opened the wardrobe. She saw a golden yellow ball gown with matching shoes and handbag. She put on her ball gown. As she wore the magical dress, her hair did itself up in a new style and makeup adorned her face. She was even wearing golden yellow gemstone jewellery. She was unrecognizable because of her beautiful appearance. Her dress, shoes, handbag, and hairstyle were in perfect combination. Her makeup was radiant, allowing her beauty to shine through flawlessly.

She went into the stable and opened the door. The carriage was waiting for her. Everything in perfect order. One of the riders of the carriage smiled to Juliana and said, "Greetings from your grandmother in the sky."

She smiled back and thought of her grandmother and was filled with gratitude. She took a deep breath to calm down. She was ready to go to the ball.

The invited guests watched her with admiration as she entered the ballroom. Her presence fascinated the guests at the ball. She radiated like sunshine. Her eyes searched for Armando. She didn't know that all other eyes were directed at her. She greeted everyone gracefully. The music played on.

She recognized the charming lord, and her heart began pounding. There was a great attraction between them. They couldn't keep their eyes off each other. They danced for hours.

It was as if the dance music had been composed for Juliana and Armando. It was as if the ball had been organized just for them. The atmosphere was so magical that everyone stopped dancing and watched the two of them as spectators. It was like a fairytale.

The lord was fascinated by her golden yellow appearance.

After dancing, they went to the balcony to enjoy the night atmosphere under the stars.

"My love is as pure as the rays of the stars, as the appearance of the sun, as the beauty of nature," he said to her. "I have a gift for you," said the lord to Juliana. He gave her a hairpin with three gemstones: a red diamond, a green diamond, and a blue diamond. Juliana looked at her hairpin and found it so wonderful that a smile spread across her face.

"It's so beautiful," she said, and she thanked him.

"These gemstones have a meaning," he said. "The red diamond designates love, the green diamond designates health, and the blue diamond designates freedom."

He was aware of the value of love because the hump on his back taught him to fall in love with a soul. He was aware of the value of health because he had intense pain during the day from the hump on his back. He was aware of the value of freedom because he could not walk straight during the day due to the hump on his back.

He placed the hairpin with gemstones in her hair and whispered in her ear, "Your beauty is more valuable than all the diamonds."

Juliana felt happy with his compliment.

The lord felt that he no longer needed anything more than what he had.

"I have no more greed. Our love is enough for me," he said. He emphasized his words with a kiss on her lips. It was as if the love angel, Cupid, shot an arrow from his bow of love at their hearts.

The hours flew past in each other's company, and soon it was time to leave.

At the end of the ball, they said goodbye to each other reluctantly. They agreed to see each other again at the next ball. During the departure, the lord kissed the lips of Juliana, full of desire. He was in love with her. The stars in the sky witnessed their lovers' kiss.

It was like a dream come true for Juliana. She was in love with him and he with her. She felt happy. She had listened to her grandmother's love fairytales so many times. She did not know that falling in love was so great until she had fallen in love. She thought that love existed only in fairy tales. The love she felt for the lord of the castle made her sure that love existed in real life too.

"This is such a beautiful hairpin," she said as she looked at the mirror at her home. She put her ball gown and accessories, such as shoes and handbag, back in the wardrobe.

The next day, the lord woke up without his hunchback. He was speechless with surprise. Suddenly, the good fairy appeared with a smile and said to him, "You have had luck. Be aware of the value of your love."

The lord was liberated from the curse. He thought about Juliana.

***

In the morning, bringing coffee to the working room of the castle was one of Juliana's tasks. This morning, in her excitement, she didn't dare to look to the lord. As a result, she didn't notice that he had no hump on his back today. She put his coffee on his desk without looking at him and turned back to the door to leave.

The lord took his cup and watched the servant. He noted something remarkable. Her hairpin was the gift that he had given Juliana at the ball. She had forgotten to remove the gift she had received from the lord.

He did not know the first name of this servant. So far, he had not asked her name, not finding it important.

He called her, "Juliana."

She turned back and looked at him, making herself known by responding to her name. Her heart was pounding; she felt as if it would fly from her chest.

He went up to her and looked at her.

"Juliana, when I look in your eyes, I forget who I am. I love you."

Juliana felt happy.

"I love you too," she said. They embraced each other with desire and passion.

They were so happy that no words could express how lucky they felt. The look in their eyes said how dearly they loved each other.

The lord adjusted the rents of the fields, and the farmers were relieved that they could now afford to pay. They cheered with joy.

Juliana and Armando married and lived happily in the castle for a long time.

About the Author

Ayşenur Akgöz is born in Turkey. When she was a child, she immigrated to Belgium, where she studied from third to sixth grade and attended secondary school. She took her high study in the Netherlands. Her hobbies are reading and jogging in the open air. She loves horses.

About the Book

A greedy lord is punished by a fairy. He can be delivered from his curse by only one condition. If you are curious about what his redemption will entail, read this fairy tale. Whatever your age, enjoy this fairy tale! You will not regret it.

Printed in the United States
By Bookmasters